JAZZ BANDS
Ruth Daly
BANDS
LET'S READ
AV2
BY WEIGL™
ADDED VALUE • AUDIO VISUAL
www.av2books.com

Go to www.av2books.com, and enter this book's unique code.

BOOK CODE

AVV67795

AV² by Weigl brings you media enhanced books that support active learning.

AV² provides enriched content that supplements and complements this book. Weigl's AV² books strive to create inspired learning and engage young minds in a total learning experience.

Your AV² Media Enhanced books come alive with...

Audio
Listen to sections of the book read aloud.

Video
Watch informative video clips.

Embedded Weblinks
Gain additional information for research.

Try This!
Complete activities and hands-on experiments.

Key Words
Study vocabulary, and complete a matching word activity.

Quizzes
Test your knowledge.

Slide Show
View images and captions, and prepare a presentation.

... and much, much more!

Published by AV² by Weigl
350 5th Avenue, 59th Floor New York, NY 10118
Website: www.av2books.com

Library of Congress Control Number: 2019938593

ISBN 978-1-7911-1126-7 (hardcover)
ISBN 978-1-7911-1127-4 (softcover)
ISBN 978-1-7911-1128-1 (multi-user eBook)
ISBN 978-1-7911-1129-8 (single-user eBook)

Printed in Guangzhou, China
1 2 3 4 5 6 7 8 9 0 23 22 21 20 19

062019
311018

Project Coordinator: Heather Kissock Designer: Terry Paulhus

Weigl acknowledges Getty Images, Alamy, Shutterstock, and iStock as the primary image suppliers for this title.

CONTENTS

In this book, you will learn about

Saxophones honk.
The piano tinkles.

The music is loud.
Jazz bands are fun.

Jazz bands get people moving. Some dance. Others tap their feet in time. Jazz bands make people feel joy.

NATCHEZ.
STEAMER
NATCHEZ

Jazz bands started in America more than 100 years ago. The first bands appeared in New Orleans. Some bands played on riverboats.

Louis Armstrong was a popular singer and trumpet player. He started playing jazz music in New Orleans. He played in many jazz bands.

Louis Armstrong sometimes played **300 concerts** a year.

Jazz musicians take turns playing alone. This is called a solo. Solos let each musician shine.

Trumpets and trombones often play the loudest part of a song.

The drums and bass keep a steady beat.

The **piccolo trumpet** is the **smallest** trumpet. It can be played with one hand.

TORINO JAZZ FESTIVAL

The bandleader tells the band when to start playing. This person sometimes plays an instrument, too.

Jazz bands perform at festivals. They play in jazz halls, too. Some bands take part in competitions.

More than **145 jazz festivals** are held in the United States every year.

TRADITIONAL 1.00
OTHERS $2.00
SAINTS $5.00
JAZZ
BAND

The New Orleans Jazz and Heritage Festival takes place every spring. Many jazz bands play there. Thousands of people come to hear jazz played live.

ACURA
NEW ORLEANS JAZZ & HERITAGE FESTIVAL
JAZZ FEST
ACURA
Jazz Tent

See what you have learned about jazz bands.

Which of these pictures is not a jazz band?

TRADITIONAL
OTHERS 2.00
SAINTS 5.00
JAZZ
BAND

KEY WORDS

Research has shown that as much as 65 percent of all written material published in English is made up of 300 words. These 300 words cannot be taught using pictures or learned by sounding them out. They must be recognized by sight. This book contains 55 common sight words to help young readers improve their reading fluency and comprehension. This book also teaches young readers several important content words, such as proper nouns. These words are paired with pictures to aid in learning and improve understanding.

Page	Sight Words First Appearance
4	the
5	are, is
7	feet, get, in, make, others, people, some, their, time
9	America, first, more, on, started, than, years
10	a, and, he, many, sometimes, was
13	each, let, take, this, turns
14	be, can, hand, it, keep, of, often, one, part, play, song, with
17	an, tells, to, too, when
18	at, every, they
20	come, hear, live, place, there

Page	Content Words First Appearance
4	piano, saxophones
5	jazz bands, music
7	joy
9	New Orleans, riverboats
10	concerts, Louis Armstrong, player, singer, trumpet
13	musicians, solo
14	bass, beat, drums, hand, piccolo, trombones
17	bandleader, instrument
18	competitions, festivals, halls, spring, United States

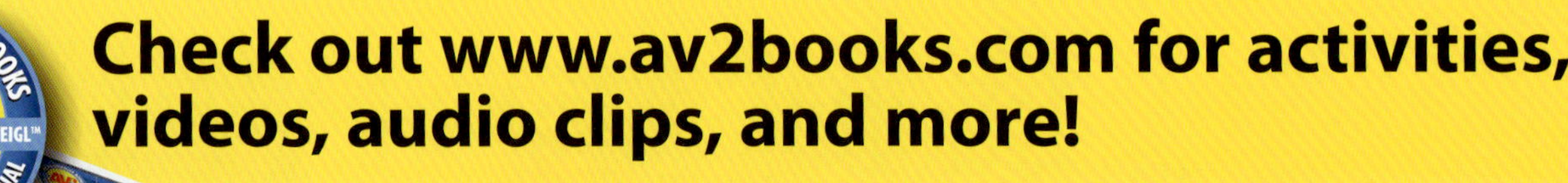

1 Go to www.av2books.com.

2 Enter book code. AVV67795

3 Fuel your imagination online!

www.av2books.com